For the Moore boys, the Branscombe-Ross boys, and all the other boys

who know what it means to have and to be a *No-Matter-What* Friend—KLW

To all my friends, no matter why—PP

Published by Tradewind Books in Canada and the UK in 2014
Text copyright © 2014 Kari-Lynn Winters
Illustrations copyright © 2014 Pierre Pratt

LIBRARY AND ARCHIVES CANADA CATALOGUING IN PUBLICATION

Winters, Kari-Lynn, 1969-, author
   No-matter-what friend / written by Kari-Lynn Winters
; illusrated by Pierre Pratt.

ISBN 978-1-896580-83-8 (bound)

   I. Pratt, Pierre, illustrator II. Title.

PS8645.I5745N6 2014   jC813'.6   C2013-907461-9

Cataloguing and publication data available from the British Library

Book design by Elisa Gutiérrez

10 9 8 7 6 5 4 3 2 1

Printed in Canada by Friesens on FSC ®
certified paper using vegetable-based inks.

The publisher thanks the Government of Canada and Canadian
Heritage for their financial support through the Canada Council
for the Arts, the Canada Book Fund and Livres Canada Books.
The publisher also thanks the Government of the Province of
British Columbia for the financial support it has given through
the Book Publishing Tax Credit program and the British
Columbia Arts Council.

No-Matter-What Friend

Written by
KARI-LYNN WINTERS

Illustrations by
PIERRE PRATT

Tradewind Books
VANCOUVER • LONDON

Old dog.

Sleepy dog.

What do you see

when you lift your lazy lids and look at me?

Do you see me and think, "That's my boy!"
Do you watch me and wonder, "Wasn't that MY toy?"

Do you wish that things were like they used to be?

And no matter what . . .

. . . you were there for me.

Remember the times we chased Dad's truck?

And last summer when you pulled me out of the muck?

I laughed when you shook,

spraying Mom with mud.

Want to run with me now?
C'mere, Bud.

No wait, Bud.

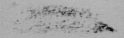

Stop.

Sit.

Stay.

Old dog, sweet dog,
I hope that you see
a no-matter-what friend
when you look at me.

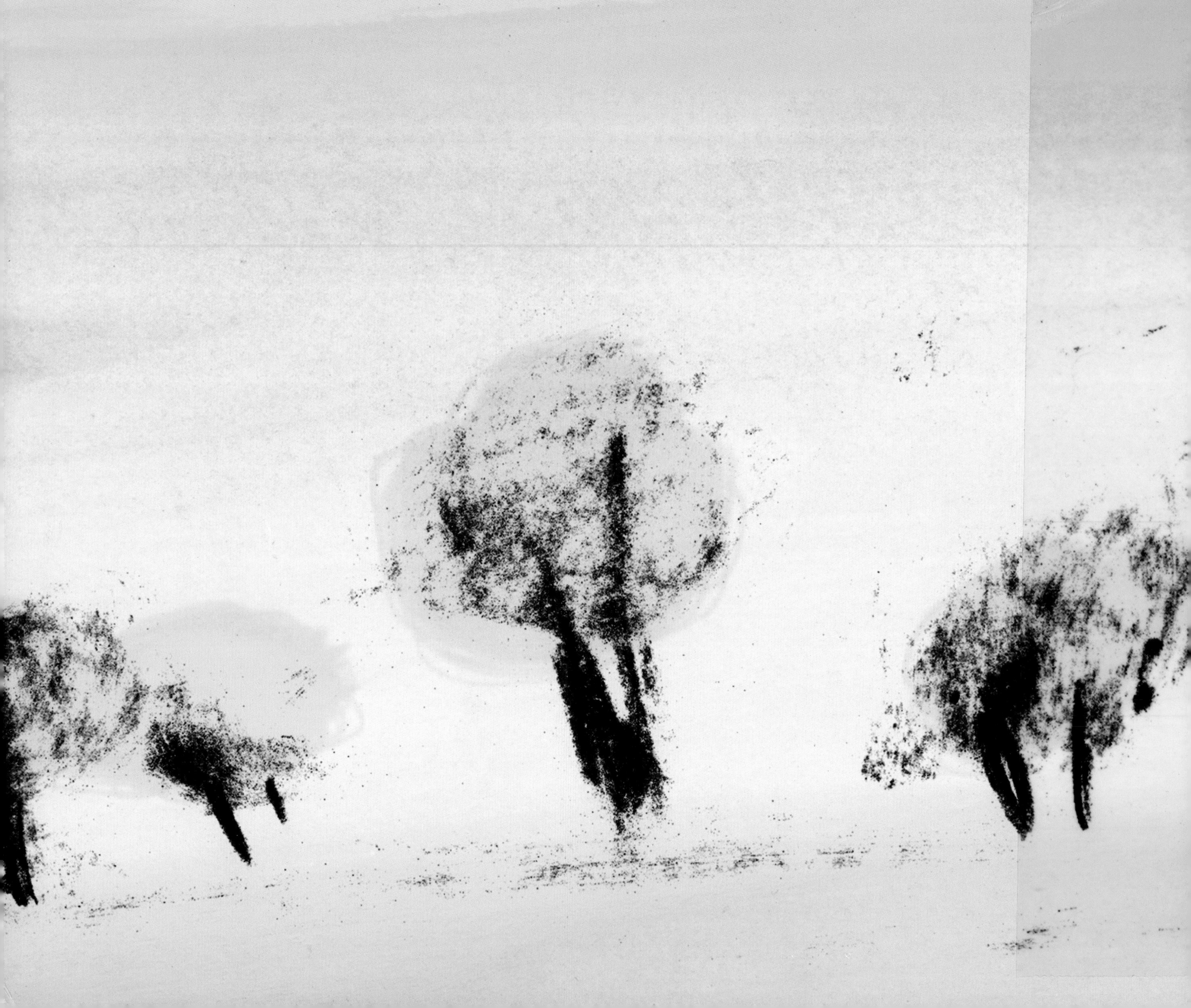